A Peach Street Mudders Story

D0107376

Shadow Over Second

by Matt Christopher

Illustrated by Anna Dewdney

Little, Brown and Company

Boston   New York   London

To Stephanie True Peters

Text copyright © 1996 by Catherine M. Christopher
Illustrations copyright © 1996 by Anna Dewdney

First Edition

The characters and events portrayed in this book are fictitious.
Any similarity to real persons, living or dead, is coincidental
and not intended by the author.

Matt Christopher™ is a trademark of Catherine M. Christopher.

Library of Congress Cataloging-in-Publication Data

Christopher, Matt.
    Shadow over second : a Peach Street Mudders story / by
Matt Christopher ; illustrated by Anna Dewdney. — 1st ed.
        p.   cm.
    Summary: Nicky is on his way to breaking the record for
most runs batted in, but first he must overcome his supersti-
tions, and someone who doesn't want to see the old record
broken.
    ISBN 0-316-14078-3 (hc) ISBN 0-316-14204-2 (pb)
    [1. Baseball — Fiction.   2. Superstition — Fiction.]
I. Dewdney, Anna, ill.   II. Title.
PZ7.C458Sf   1996
[Fic] — dc20   95-36024

10 9 8 7 6 5 4 3 2

COM-MO

PRINTED IN THE UNITED STATES OF AMERICA

1

"STEEE-RIKE!" boomed the ump as Bucky Neal breezed in a pitch past T.V. Adams.

"C'mon, T.V.," Nicky Chong muttered. He was on deck. There were two outs, and it was the top of the third inning. "Save me a rap."

Nicky had good reason to want another time at bat this game. He had doubled his first time up and hoped to do it again this time. And if he did, he stood a good chance of leading the league in runs batted in.

Maybe that record wasn't as glamorous as hitting the most home runs or pitching a no-hitter. But it was a record he knew he would be proud to hold. And he was only six RBIs away from making it.

"Steee-rike two!" the umpire called.

"Oh, no!" Nicky moaned. "What're you waiting for, T.V.?"

T.V. had struck out the first time up, and it looked as if he was heading down that same route again. So far the score was Mudders 1, Green Dragons 0. A single from T.V. would put José Mendez on second. And if Nicky was the man to bat José home, he'd be one RBI closer to his record.

The next pitch was a knee-high blazer. "Swing!" Nicky muttered. T.V. did, and belted a sizzling grounder to third.

"Good shot!" Nicky yelled. The Dragons' third baseman bobbled the ball, then recovered and whipped it to second. José was safe! Second baseman Dale Emerson relayed to first. T.V. was safe by a step!

Nicky picked up a bat. But he didn't go directly to the batter's box. He went through a ritual he performed each time he prepared to bat.

First he tapped his right foot with the bat. Then his left. Then he took two swings. Finally he stepped into the batter's box and touched the outside left corner with the bat, then the right. Only then did he face the pitcher.

He let the first two pitches go by for balls, then swung at the third — and sent it soaring over the fence for a home run! He was a third of the way to first base before he tossed the bat aside.

Worked again! he thought with glee. *That ol' ritual hasn't failed me yet this season!*

The Mudders' fans cheered loudly. As Nicky trotted over home plate, the team was waiting to congratulate him.

"Way to go, Nicky!" called T.V. Adams. "Three more runs for the Mudders! And you're that much closer to you-know-what!"

Nicky smiled and took a seat on the bench. But secretly he wished T.V. hadn't said anything. The Mudders had only two more games left this season, so breaking the record would be no easy task. And like many ball-players, Nicky was superstitious. He was afraid that talking about his chances might jinx him.

Just to be on the safe side, he rapped his knuckles on the bench.

Knock on wood, he thought. *That should counteract T.V.'s blunder!*

2

The score still read Mudders 4, Dragons 0, when Alfie Maples popped out to third to end the Mudders' turn at bat.

The Dragons started out strong. The first batter slugged a triple into right field. A moment later, he crossed home plate on a single by Eddie Kolski.

"That's enough!" Nicky yelled from his second base position. "Let's buckle down and get them out!"

The infield chatter must have helped. The next two batters got out on a pop-up and a strikeout. Then T.V. gloved a hot bouncer to third. He pegged it to second for the forced out.

Mudders 4, Dragons 1.

"All right! How about some hits, team!" shouted Coach Parker. "Start it off, Bus!"

Bus didn't. Neither did Rudy or Sparrow. As a matter of fact, neither the Mudders nor the Dragons scored again until the last inning.

Nicky was first up at the top of the sixth. *Tap, tap, swing, swing, touch, touch,* he murmured to himself.

Bucky Neal threw the first pitch — and Nicky connected for a scorching shot over the shortstop's head! The ball bounded out to the left center field fence before Greg Barnes scooped it up and whipped it to third. Nicky wisely held up at second.

"Boy, are you having a hot day!" said Dale Emerson, the Dragons' second baseman. "Are you going for a record or something?"

Nicky just smiled and shrugged. Although Dale hadn't *specifically* mentioned the RBI record, answering might ruin his luck.

Nicky watched Alfie Maples walk on four pitches. Then Bus Mercer hit a solid single, loading the bases. Rudy Calhoun struck out, but Sparrow Fisher singled. Nicky took off from third the minute he heard the bat connect with the ball. He crossed home plate safely, adding another run to their score.

Bus wasn't as lucky. Sparrow's single was close to second base. Dale Emerson stepped on the bag seconds before Bus slid in. Bus wiped the dust from his pants and jogged off the field.

With runners on first and third, Barry McGee, the Mudders' strongest hitter, stepped to the plate. Nicky cheered him on with the rest of the Mudders' bench.

Much to everyone's surprise, Barry failed to connect with Bucky's pitches. He struck out.

The scoreboard read Mudders 5, Dragons 1.

"Okay, Sparrow," said Nicky as he passed the Mudders' pitcher on his way to second base. "The sooner you strike 'em out, the sooner we can get home!"

"And the sooner I can get some dinner in my empty stomach!" called Turtleneck Jones from first base. He patted his belly.

Nicky laughed. "I thought I heard something growl at me earlier. Hey," he added. "Speaking of growling, come by my house later on and I'll show you something really neat."

"What is it?" Turtleneck asked curiously.

"You'll see."

Both boys turned their attention to the game. Sparrow breezed in three pitches to Andy Jackson, all balls. Then he laced two pitches chest-high and over the middle of the plate. The count was now 3 and 2.

"Bear down, Sparrow!" Nicky encouraged. "Just one more!"

Sparrow twirled the ball around and around in his hand. Then he stretched and delivered.

Crack! A high, long shot toward right field! Alfie Maples took off after it, but he didn't stand a chance. It was going . . . going . . . It was gone! A home run!

3

"That's okay!" called Coach Parker from the dugout. "Don't let it shake you, Sparrow!"

That homer put the Dragons within three runs of the Mudders, reminding Nicky that as long as the Dragons were at bat, they could come out on top.

Nicky pounded his glove and crouched, ready to field anything that came near him. But Cush Boochie, the next man up, didn't give him a chance. Cush singled over short.

Beans Malone stepped to the plate.

"C'mon, Sparrow! Get 'em outta there!" Nicky yelled.

Sparrow did. He fanned Beans on three straight pitches.

That took the wind out of the Dragons' sails. Lefty Cash and Bucky Neal met the ball, but only to squeak out little dribblers. Bus easily fielded the first one and made a clean throw to Turtleneck for the second out. Nicky did the same with Bucky's hit. The game ended with the Peach Street Mudders beating the Dragons 5 to 2.

The Mudders gathered in the dugout, slapping each other on the back and exchanging high fives.

"Some fine hitting there today, Nicky," Coach Parker said. He gave Nicky a meaningful look but said nothing more. Nicky smiled gratefully. He knew that the coach knew about the record — and about Nicky's superstition against talking about it.

Nicky began collecting the bats and balls. Then he overheard something that made his heart stop.

"Do you know who holds the RBI record?" the Mudders' scorekeeper asked the Dragons' scorekeeper.

"Some guy named Sam Jolly. He made it three years ago."

"Well, I doubt he's going to hold it for much longer!"

Nicky bolted out of earshot and almost ran into Turtleneck Jones. "Let's get out of here!" he cried. Turtleneck looked surprised but grabbed his glove and followed Nicky off the field.

That was close, Nicky thought. *But they didn't mention my name. So I think I'll be okay.*

By the time he and Turtleneck reached their neighborhood, Nicky was feeling better. "Hey, don't forget to come over after dinner to see what's in the shed!" he reminded Turtleneck.

Turtleneck looked mystified but promised he'd be over as soon as he could.

4

Mrs. Chong had cooked a tasty dinner. Nicky was so hungry, he wolfed his meal down in no time. As he reached for the bowl to serve himself seconds, he knocked over the saltshaker.

"Whoops!" He righted the shaker, then grabbed a pinch of salt and tossed it over his shoulder. "For good luck!" he said with a grin. His mother looked at him quickly but said nothing. Nicky knew she didn't believe in superstitions. But he figured that every little bit of luck helped. Look what his batting ritual did for his hitting, after all!

After dinner, Nicky put his dishes in the dishwasher, then hurried out to the backyard. He had just pulled the peg out of the shed door's latch when he heard someone call his name.

"Hey, Nicky!"

It was Turtleneck.

"Shhh!" Nicky warned. He motioned for Turtleneck to look inside the shed.

There before them lay a big brown dog. Beside her were five little puppies, wriggling and making soft noises.

"Wow!" Turtleneck breathed. "Can I touch one?"

"If Babe Ruth lets you," Nicky said. "But move slowly so she doesn't get spooked."

Turtleneck knelt beside the dogs and carefully reached out his hand. He stroked the closest puppy, then looked up at Nicky with shining eyes.

"Its fur is so soft!" he whispered.

Nicky crouched beside him and petted Babe's head gently. "Yeah, they're pretty neat."

Babe Ruth laid a paw on Nicky's knee and gave a soft *whuff*.

The boys stayed in the shed until Mrs. Chong called them in. Reluctantly, Turtleneck stood up to go.

"Can I come again, Nicky?"

"You bet!"

Nicky slept soundly that night. When he woke up the next morning, he was full of energy.

"My, you look ready for just about anything today," his mother said at the breakfast table. "Good thing, too. Those stacks of newspapers in the garage need to be tied for recycling."

Nicky started to groan until he saw the look on her face. He quickly covered it up with a cough.

Nicky's father leaned over and whispered loudly, "She's got me mowing the front *and* back lawns. You're gettin' off easy!"

Nicky burst out laughing. "Hey, save me a four-leaf clover if you find one. I could use a little extra luck!"

Mrs. Chong shook her head at Nicky, then said, "You and your superstitions. Sometimes I think you really believe in that stuff."

Nicky knew better than to try to explain. He just followed his father out to the garage. His mother disappeared into the shed.

Half an hour later, Nicky dragged the last bundle of newspapers to the curb.

"Hey, aren't you Nicky Chong?"

Nicky looked up. A tall, lanky boy with sandy hair stood in front of him. He was straddling a mountain bike with big knobby tires. He looked familiar, but Nicky wasn't sure who he was.

"I'm Stick Jolly," the boy on the bike said. "I'm the third baseman for the Bulls. We're playing your team on Monday, aren't we?"

Just then, Nicky's father appeared, carrying one of the puppies.

"Nicky, have you seen the peg that holds the shed door closed? This little tyke was trying to make a getaway!"

Nicky shook his head. "Mom must have it. She told me she's not going to give you another chance to sneak up on her and lock her in!"

Mr. Chong laughed. "I wish I'd had my camera when I let her out! The look on her face!" The puppy gave a little yip. Mr. Chong held it up to his ear. "What's that? You're tired of being outside and you want to find your mother? Okay, off we go!"

Mr. Chong vanished around the corner of the house. Nicky turned to see Stick Jolly pedaling away.

Nicky shrugged, then followed his father around to the back of the house. He thought it was strange that Stick hadn't said goodbye. But the sight that greeted his eyes as he rounded the corner chased that thought away.

22

5

Puppies were everywhere!

"They just decided today was the day to go outside!" Mrs. Chong gasped as she ran by Nicky, scooping up a puppy with one hand while holding another under her arm. Nicky joined in the chase. Mr. Chong was nowhere to be seen.

Ten minutes later, all the runaways had been carefully returned to the shed with their mother. Mrs. Chong wedged the peg securely in place.

"Whew!" she said. She glanced sideways

at Nicky. "Thanks for your help. Your father just disappeared when he saw what had happened!"

Suddenly Nicky heard a soft laugh. He spun around to see his father walking toward them. "Well, I had to get this!" he said gaily. He waved a camera over his head. "That was the funniest thing I've seen in a while! It will be the perfect addition to the family album."

Mrs. Chong and Nicky both groaned. An *embarrassing* addition to the album, Nicky thought.

Later that afternoon, Nicky called Turtleneck to see if he wanted to play some pitch-and-catch. Turtleneck agreed to meet him at the ball field.

When they arrived, some other kids were riding their bikes around the bases. Nicky recognized Stick Jolly in the crowd.

"Hey," he called when Stick rode past

him. "Don't you know you shouldn't ride here? Your tires could really chew up the turf!"

Stick rounded first, then turned his front wheel sharply. He rode fast toward the pitcher's mound. Reaching top speed, he pulled back sharply on his handlebars and jumped over the small hump. He landed with a thud and pedaled straight at home plate — right where Nicky and Turtleneck were standing!

The two boys leapt out of the way just as Stick skidded to a stop a foot in front of them. A cloud of dust blew up from the ground and surrounded Nicky and Turtleneck. When the dust cleared, Nicky saw with dismay that Stick's tires had made a deep rut in the dirt.

"Whadja do that for?" he cried. "Someone might twist an ankle in that hole unless it's fixed before the next game!"

Stick shrugged.

"It's not my team's playing field," he said. "And since your team is playing on my field on Monday, what do you care? Someone will take care of it before you play here again, right?"

"So then you're just making work for somebody," Nicky fumed. "It's just wrong to do it — that's all."

Turtleneck nodded in agreement. "Yeah, why don't you guys ride somewhere else?"

"C'mon, Stick, let's get going," called a boy. He looked a lot like Stick but was older. In fact, all of the other bike riders looked older. "Or would you rather stay with these Goody Two-shoes than ride with us?"

Stick snorted. "No way, Sam! I'm coming!" He rode off the field and down the street with the others.

"That guy really burns me up," Turtleneck said angrily.

"Me, too," Nicky replied, staring at the

rut in the dirt at his feet. "Hey, T., let's go back to my house and get something to fix this, okay?"

"Good idea," Turtleneck said. "I'll bet we find some other places where the field is dug up, too."

Twenty minutes later, they were back with a long-handled garden rake. They took turns smoothing over the holes left behind by the bike tires. Soon the diamond looked as good as new.

The boys tossed the baseball back and forth for a while, then went back to Nicky's house to play with the puppies.

Turtleneck lay back and put a puppy on his chest. The dog wriggled for a moment, then fell asleep. "Say, Nicky, are you nervous about the game on Monday?"

Nicky's heart fluttered. "I'll just play like I usually do, I guess," he mumbled.

"Are you talking about Nicky's near-record-breaking RBI stat?" a voice boomed.

The puppy on Turtleneck's stomach woke with a start. Both boys jumped.

Mr. Chong stood in the doorway. What he said next made Nicky's heart sink to his stomach.

"Only four to go now, isn't that right? That's some impressive hitting streak, son!"

6

Nicky couldn't believe it. His *own father* had jinxed him!

But Mr. Chong didn't seem to know what he had done. "Well, never fear, you'll hear me cheering you on at the game on Monday. Your mother conned me into taking the day off. I have to put up the fence so these little guys can roam around the backyard. In fact," he added with a slow smile, "I could use two able-bodied young helpers. Any volunteers?"

He looked from boy to boy. "Hey, why so glum? It won't be that bad! Besides," he said, "you can play with the puppies!"

*   *   *

On Monday morning, Turtleneck showed up ready for work — and play. He had his base-ball glove and uniform in his backpack, since Mr. Chong had said he'd drive them to the field in the afternoon.

Nicky was nervous about the game. All the previous night, he had tried to convince himself that his father hadn't really "whammied" him. He had almost talked himself into believing it. Almost.

Mr. Chong stood beside several rolls of chain-link fence. He handed Nicky a tape measure and pointed to a pile of poles.

"We'll need to mark off spots to put the fence poles," Mr. Chong said. "Nicky, you and T. measure out a big rectangle. The house will be one side, and the shed will be the middle of the opposite side. Lay down a pole at the corners, then one every ten feet along the sides. Okay?"

Nicky and Turtleneck nodded.

"Great! Now my job is to find out which of our neighbors has a sledgehammer I can borrow to pound the posts in. Back soon!" He disappeared down the street.

Nicky and Turtleneck set to work. They crisscrossed the lawn, moving back and forth from the pile of poles to different spots on the rectangle. An hour later, the poles were scattered evenly around the yard, but Mr. Chong still hadn't returned.

Turtleneck tugged at Nicky's sleeve. "Let's go play with the puppies," he said. Nicky glanced at his watch.

"We have to be at the field in an hour for warm-up," he warned. "Maybe I should find my dad."

"We'll keep an eye on the time just in case we have to walk."

Nicky agreed. He led the way to the shed, pulled the peg out, and opened the door.

Babe Ruth and her litter rushed to meet them. Nicky quickly pulled the door shut before they could escape.

The boys rolled on the floor, tickling the puppies and having their noses and ears nipped by sharp little teeth. After a while, the puppies tired out. One by one, they fell asleep. Nicky and Turtleneck lay down beside them, being careful to keep their voices low.

"Hey, T.," Nicky whispered after a moment. "Do you — do you think I'll be okay at the game today? Or do you think my dad jinxed me?"

Turtleneck shrugged. "You're a good player, Nicky. What do you think?"

"I don't know —" Nicky's reply was cut off when Babe gave a sharp *woof* and jangled her collar. For a second, Nicky thought he heard something else, too. But the sound was gone before he could identify it.

Turtleneck sat up suddenly. "Oh, my gosh! What time is it?" he asked. Nicky checked his watch.

"Uh-oh. It's five of two," he said. "Since Dad's not back yet, I guess we should get ready and head over."

He pushed on the door to the shed.

It didn't budge!

He pushed again, harder this time. Still no movement!

"T., come here and help me!" he cried.

Both boys shoved as hard as they could. But the door stayed closed tight.

All of a sudden, Nicky stuck his hand in his pocket. "T., do you remember what I did with the peg when we came in?" he asked.

Turtleneck shook his head. They stared at each other in fear.

"Someone must have put the peg back in!" Nicky whispered hoarsely. "It's because of the jinx! Turtleneck, we're trapped!"

7

"Who would lock us in here?" Turtleneck wondered. "And why?"

All at once, Nicky remembered the strange sound he'd heard after Babe had barked. It had been so soft, he figured he had imagined it. But now he wasn't so sure. In fact, the more he thought about it, the more he was sure he had heard muffled laughter.

Suddenly Nicky was angry. He started pounding on the door and yelling with all his might.

"Dad, let us out of here! This isn't funny! Let us out right now!"

Turtleneck stared at him in amazement. "You think your dad's out there?" he asked.

"I think he did this as a *joke!*" Nicky fumed. "Boy, has he ever gone too far this time!"

The boys hammered their fists on the door together and shouted over and over to be let out. The puppies woke up and added their cries, too.

After what seemed like an eternity, the boys heard a voice on the other side of the door.

"Hold on, hold on," it said. Moments later, the door swung open. Mr. Chong stood before them, holding a camera.

"Real funny, Dad!" Nicky exploded. "But you're not going to add *this* moment to the family album!"

Nicky and Turtleneck rushed down the shed ramp. Just as they reached the bottom, Nicky's foot caught on something. He stumbled and almost fell, but didn't. He glanced

back to see what he had tripped over. There was a deep groove in the grass. Nicky frowned, but Turtleneck's voice interrupted his thoughts.

"C'mon, Nicky, shake a leg!"

The boys scrambled into their uniforms while Mr. Chong pulled the car out into the driveway. Mrs. Chong was seated beside him, looking worried. They jumped into the backseat, and the car sped off.

"Nicky, I don't know what you're thinking, but —," Mr. Chong began.

Nicky blurted, "I'll tell you what I'm thinking! I'm thinking that thanks to you, I'll never break that RBI record!"

"Nicky!" exclaimed Turtleneck, horrified.

"Talking about it can't hurt anything now, T.," Nicky grumbled. "The damage is done."

Mrs. Chong looked over her shoulder. "Nicky, we'll explain everything to Coach Parker. I'm sure he'll let you in the game."

"That won't matter," Nicky replied bitterly. "I'm not going to get a hit anyway. Even if Dad hadn't locked us in the shed —"

Her eyes blazing, Mrs. Chong spun around in her seat. "You think your *father* locked you in the shed?"

Nicky crossed his arms over his chest. "All I know is that when the door opened, there was Dad. With his camera. But it really doesn't matter if he was the one who did it or not. He jinxed me, and the jinx is coming true. Dark forces are working to keep me from reaching the RBI record."

Mrs. Chong narrowed her eyes. " 'Jinxed you'? *'Dark forces'*? That's it! Nicky, this superstitious nonsense has gone on long enough! Do you seriously believe anything your father — or anyone — says can cause you bad luck?"

Nicky sat in stony silence.

His mother sighed. "Nicky, if you don't

get a hit this game, it won't be because of something your father said. It will be because you think superstition counts more than your ability! Now, promise me that you'll put this silly jinx idea right out of your head!"

Nicky locked eyes with her for a moment. Then he nodded once.

"And as for you," she continued, turning her gaze to Mr. Chong. "Why exactly were you holding your camera? And what happened to the sledgehammer?"

Mr. Chong raised an eyebrow. "The sledgehammer is in our garage. And I was holding the camera because I had just reloaded it. I plan to take a whole roll of pictures of today's game."

Nicky sank lower into his seat. He felt like a heel for accusing his father.

But if his father hadn't locked the shed, who had?

8

When they reached the baseball diamond, the game was already in progress. The Mudders were at bat in the top of the second inning, with the score at Stockade Bulls 2, Peach Street Mudders 0. The boys rushed to join their teammates.

"What happened to you guys?" Barry McGee said. "Forget we had a game this afternoon?"

"We sure could use your stick, Nicky," added T.V. Adams.

"Thanks, T.V.," Nicky said. *But even if the coach lets me play, I'm not sure I'll be much help,* he added silently.

"Nicky! Turtleneck! Come here!" Coach Parker called.

Uh-oh, Nicky thought. *Here it comes.*

"Your mom has explained what happened, Nicky," Coach Parker said. "Since your tardiness wasn't your fault, I see no reason why you and Turtleneck shouldn't play. Go warm up."

Nicky's heart soared. He and Turtleneck exchanged high fives, and the rest of the Mudders cheered. Only one person, substitute player Jack Livingston, looked disappointed.

That look made a strange thought cross Nicky's mind.

Could Jack have wanted to play so badly that *he* locked the shed?

As soon as he thought it, Nicky knew he was pointing fingers at the wrong guy. Jack might not be the best player, but he was a good kid who wanted the Mudders to win as much as his teammates did.

Well, now I know two people who didn't *lock us in,* Nicky thought. *But that doesn't tell me who* did.

He pushed the thought from his mind. Now was not the time to think about anything but the game. He pulled his cap low over his eyes and turned his attention to the batter.

Zero Ford was pitching for the Mudders this game, with Chess Laveen behind the plate. Phil Koline, the Bulls' right fielder, led off. Zero threw the first pitch.

Strike one!

"Way to go, Zero!" Turtleneck yelled from first base. "Two more like it!"

But Zero couldn't seem to find the plate for the next three pitches. The count rose to 3 and 1.

Then Phil drilled a pitch to deep right center. He pulled up on second for a double.

One man on, no outs.

The Bulls' next batter tried to bunt the first

pitch. The ball rolled foul just left of the third base line marker. Strike one.

He tried it again — and missed again. Strike two.

The Bulls' coach must have told him to swing away at the third pitch. But instead of hitting the ball, he fanned. One out.

The Mudders' fans cheered.

Next up was Adzie Healy, the Bulls' center fielder. He took three pitches — two balls and a strike — then flew out to left.

"One more, Zero!" Nicky cried. "One more, buddy!"

The next batter strode to the plate. Nicky recognized him at once. It was Stick Jolly.

"C'mon, Stick, show 'em what you've got!" yelled a voice from the Bulls' stands. It sounded familiar to Nicky. Sure enough, Stick's brother, Sam, was in the bleachers.

Seeing him made something in Nicky's mind click. But before he could work out just what it was, he heard the crack of the bat hitting the ball. Hard.

It was coming right to him! Nicky backed up a step, held his glove up in the air — and caught the ball for the third out!

The Mudders' bench erupted with cheers. But Nicky just tossed the ball aside and jogged off the field, his head low.

There's some reason I've heard of Stick's brother, he thought. *But what?*

He just couldn't remember.

Barry McGee was first up for the Mudders at the top of the third inning. He stepped to the plate and on the very first pitch, knocked in a double between short and third.

"Okay, Turtleneck," Coach Parker called. "Show 'em your stuff!"

Turtleneck socked a line drive that smacked into the pitcher's glove — then bounced out again! He was safely on first by the time the pitcher recovered the ball. Barry hadn't moved from second.

After Turtleneck came José Mendez. José wasn't the strongest hitter, but sometimes he could surprise you.

This time it was the ball that surprised everyone. José hit it right toward third base, but it took a funny bounce toward second. Barry, Turtleneck, and José ran as fast as they could. But only Barry and José were left on the diamond at the end of the play. The second baseman had beaten Turtleneck to the bag, and he was out.

Two players on base, one out.

Nicky knelt in the on-deck circle, watching T.V. take a few practice swings. His heart was thumping.

This is it, he thought. *Even if T.V. gets out, I'll have a chance to make an RBI. I could bat Barry home.*

T.V. swung at three pitches. He missed three times.

Two outs.

Nicky stood up. He was about to go

through his pre-batting ritual when he remembered his promise to his mother.

Oh, man, he thought.

9

"Batter up!" the umpire called. "C'mon, son, time's ticking."

Reluctantly Nicky stepped into the box.

Here goes nothing, he thought dismally.

But when the pitcher reared back and threw, Nicky's instincts took over. He swung. Hard.

Crack!

A high-flying ball straight into the hole behind the shortstop! Nicky's cleats tore up the dirt as he hightailed it to first.

Safe!

A loud cheer rose from the Mudders' fans. It got even louder when Barry McGee beat the throw to home.

The score now read Bulls 2, Mudders 1. And Nicky knew that the scorekeeper was placing a small, neat check mark in the RBI column next to his name.

One down, three to go, he thought, dazed. *Maybe I'm not jinxed after all! Or maybe Mom's right,* he added. *Maybe superstitious rituals have less to do with my hitting than I think!*

A moment later, Alfie Maples popped out to end the Mudders' turn at bat.

The Bulls' second baseman led off at the bottom of the third. He drilled a low pitch to deep right. It sailed between José and Alfie and went for a triple.

Adzie Healy drew a walk, Stick Jolly fanned, and Jim Hance singled. Bases loaded.

"C'mon, Zero, use your magic touch!" T.V. shouted from third base.

Zero did. He struck out the next batter. Then Turtleneck caught a fly ball. Three outs.

The Mudders could do nothing their turn at bat, and the Bulls came up still ahead by one run. By the end of the inning, they had added two more runs to their lead. Bulls 4, Mudders 1.

The fifth inning saw no change in the score. In fact, both teams brought three batters to the plate and watched three batters return without getting on base.

The Mudders started off the sixth and last inning at the top of the order. Once again, Nicky watched T.V. from the on-deck circle. T.V. hit a solid single.

Nicky stood and marched straight into the batter's box.

Okay, Mom, a promise is a promise, he thought, gritting his teeth. *But let's see if that first hit was just a fluke.*

What happened next made Nicky question forevermore the value of superstition. He swung at the first pitch — and connected so hard that the bat cracked in two! He didn't

wait to see the pieces land. He just ran as fast as he could. When he stopped, he was standing on third base.

Nicky had chalked up another RBI. The score now read Bulls 4, Mudders 2.

The cheers that burst forth from the stands were deafening. Even if the Mudders didn't win the game, Nicky was sure the fans would go home happy. His grin was so wide, it almost split his face in half.

But then he heard a noise that wiped the smile from his lips.

It was a low laugh. So low it sounded muffled.

He spun around and found himself face to face with Stick Jolly.

"Bet you thought that RBI was going to help your stupid team pull ahead, didn't you?" Stick said. "Well, guess again!"

Nicky was stunned. Stick's words were hateful. But it was his laugh that had jolted him. He had heard that laugh earlier that day — *only moments before he and Turtleneck had discovered themselves locked in the shed!*

10

But if that were true, Nicky told himself, *then Stick must be the one who put the peg into the latch!*

Then Nicky hesitated. Was a barely heard laugh enough evidence to accuse someone of sabotage?

As Alfie Maples stepped to the plate for his turn at bat, Nicky replayed the morning's events over again in his mind: from the time he and Turtleneck walked into the shed, to when Babe Ruth barked, to when they discovered they'd been locked in, to when Mr. Chong had freed them. . . .

Suddenly, clear as a bell, Nicky saw himself running down the shed ramp — *and tripping over a rut in the grass!* But he and Turtleneck had been back and forth across the lawn countless times that morning. Not once had Nicky noticed anything strange about the ground around the shed.

More important, he knew he had seen a rut like that once before. It was just like the one he and Turtleneck had repaired in the baseball diamond after Stick Jolly had ridden his bike on it!

It was you! he wanted to shout. *You're the one!*

But he didn't. Something was still missing. What motive could Stick have to lock the shed with Nicky and Turtleneck inside? That was a question Nicky just couldn't answer.

Alfie struck out his turn at bat. Then Bus sent a streaking grounder through short. It was enough to score Nicky, but not enough to win the Mudders the game. As Nicky watched from the Mudders' bench, Chess Laveen popped up to end the sixth inning. The final score was Bulls 4, Mudders 2.

"Okay, fellas, let's line up and shake hands," Coach Parker called. Nicky joined his teammates. He automatically murmured "Good game" to each of the Bulls' players.

When he got to Stick, he hesitated, then stuck out his hand. Stick took it. As he did, he glanced over his shoulder at his brother, Sam, and gave a sly smile.

Suddenly Nicky's memory came flooding back. He knew what it was about Sam Jolly that had been nagging at his brain since the start of the game. It was something he had overheard a few days ago.

Sam Jolly, Stick's older brother, was the person who held the record for most RBIs — the very record Nicky was closing in on! What better reason would Stick need to keep Nicky from the game?

Nicky tightened his grip on Stick's hand.

Stick's eyes widened. Nicky stared at him, then said in a low voice, "I know what you did, Stick. And I think it stinks."

Stick tore his hand free. "I don't know what you're talking about," he said. But he couldn't meet Nicky's gaze.

The lines of players had stopped moving when Nicky did. Now the two teams gathered around Nicky and Stick. Turtleneck pushed his way next to Nicky.

"T., take a good look at the guy who locked us in the shed today," Nicky said. Turtleneck's eyebrows shot up.

"What's going on here?" Coach Parker asked. The Bulls' coach appeared beside him.

Nicky took a deep breath. "Coach, Stick Jolly is the reason Turtleneck and I were late to today's game. He locked us in my shed. We would probably still be in there if my dad hadn't let us out."

"You can't prove I did that!" Stick cried.

"I think I can," Nicky said. He explained

about the rut in the grass and the muffled laugh. "I figure he was trying to prevent me from breaking his brother's RBI record," he concluded.

The Bulls' coach laid a heavy hand on Stick's shoulder. "Well, son?" he asked. "The truth, now."

Stick hung his head. "Yeah, I did it," he whispered. "I got the idea from your dad that day your puppies got loose. I knew you were superstitious — I've seen that ritual you go through before you bat and all — and I overheard you and Turtleneck talking about it, too, just before I put the peg in the shed latch. So I figured, even if you did get out in time for the game, you'd think you'd been jinxed and wouldn't play well." He grimaced. "I guess it was pretty dumb, but that record is important to my brother. I-I'm sorry, Nicky."

Nicky was quiet for a moment. Then he slowly extended his hand. "No hard feelings,

Stick," he said. The boys shook hands.

Suddenly Nicky grinned. "But let me tell you right now," he said, "I'm only one away from that record — and I've got a sneaking suspicion I'm going to break it! I'm going to concentrate on playing, not on worrying about being jinxed. No more superstitious nonsense for me!"

Turtleneck punched him lightly in the shoulder. "Does that mean you're not going to do this anymore?"

He picked up a bat and mimicked Nicky's batting ritual perfectly. The Mudders all exploded with laughter.

Nicky grinned. "Well," he said, scratching his head. "Maybe I'll keep just *one* of my superstitions! After all, it's worked for me so far!"